MY DAD I

ELEVATOR!

By David Roth
Drawings by Wes Tyrell

Gunner Books

MY DAD IS AN ELEVATOR!

ISBN: 978-1-5350-9480-1

First published in 2016 by Gunner Books.

Text © 2016 David Roth. Illustrations © 2016 Wes Tyrell.

David Roth and Wes Tyrell have asserted their rights

to be identified as the author and illustrator of this work.

All enquires should be sent to gunnerbooks@gmail.com

My name is
Billy Lifft.

My Dad's name
is Otis.

He and I
are best friends.

We do
everything together!

It doesn't mean I don't love
my Mom just as much —
I really do!

It's just that my Dad
is a special person
in my life.

My Dad works a lot, but when he is around he plays with me all the time. He pushes me on the swings —

— he's teaching me how to play baseball,

and once when he knew my Mom was away
he even showed me how to climb a tree!

The one thing I like most is when my Dad and I play **ELEVATOR!**

He starts off standing tall over me and looks down and says –

And then he bends down grabbing my arms
and slowly starts to lift me up in the air,
calling out the floors as I rise!

That night as Billy lay in bed he saw a strong light shining through the window.

"Dad, what's that light coming into my room?"

Billy's dad told him the words to say
and then said goodnight.
He repeated the words many times so that
he could remember them.

Full moon...
shining....

He then went to the
window and gazed up
into the night sky.

"Full moon shining oh so bright,
I'm allowed one wish upon your sight,
One choice is mine, no less, no more,
I wish my dad were...an elevator!"

In the morning the sun was shining. It was a new day. Billy had forgotten about the wish he had made the night before.

"Hey mom, where's dad?"
"Why your father is where he always is Billy. He's at work in his office building."
"When will he be home?"
"My that's a strange question....I'm not sure."
"Can we go see him today?"
"OK, why not?"

We went into the lobby and I couldn't
believe my eyes, my Dad was an elevator!
My wish had come true!

My Dad is very important!
He lifts people to their jobs every day.

Even though my Dad is now an elevator
he still has time to coach me in sports –

and he listens patiently as I practice my reading.

I play my Zooplehorn for him so he can see
how much I've improved.

"For career day, Dad couldn't come to school, so I brought my class to him."

But being an elevator is not as easy as I thought!
My Dad has to work really hard to lift sometimes –

and some people are really stinky!

He gets very strange visitors that
even pinch his nose!

And hairy cats that stray
much too close!

We make sure that Dad is included
in all important things.

"But it's still very sad to leave every day and know that Dad can't come home with us."

In the morning Billy woke up.
He missed his Dad.

Billy ran outside to his Dad
who turned and said –
"I am an elevator.
What floor sir?"

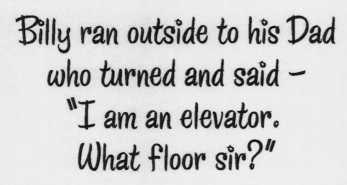

Billy jumped into his Dad's arms
and smiled –
"no, you are just my Dad
and I like that best
of all."

THE END

41291350R00020

Made in the USA
Middletown, DE
05 April 2019